MY DEAD FLOWERS

THAYIL EDITIONS

Soliloquies | Adil Jussawalla

FORTHCOMING

happily ever after | Kamal Trilok Singh

Let the Smithereens | Karthika Naïr

damn you / a magazine of the arts: Facsimile Edition | Edited by Alok Rai, Arvind Krishna Mehrotra, Amit Rai

You've Come to the Right Place | Joshua Muyiwa

PRAISE FOR *MY DEAD FLOWERS*

'There is a kind of book in which the world tilts a little. Objects glow longer than they should. Time frays at the edges, as if seen through long exposures. Small domestic incidents take on the weight of omens. *My Dead Flowers* is that kind of book. Out of hospital wards and balconies, lists and prayers, late-night messages and morning walks in Calcutta, New York and Paris, Buku Sarkar builds a household of ghosts—not only the dead, but also past selves, lost streets, mislaid countries; people who slipped away without quite leaving. Here, text and image share the same breath. A prayer. A memory. A sudden flare of pain. A joke over parsley in the kitchen. On the facing page, a blurred figure crossing a dark room, clutching something to her chest. A list of keys, dresses, spoons, apartments, husbands, passports. A life packed and repacked across continents. A train window crowded with faces. Handwriting flooding the glass, so the city turns to mist. A leafless tree spoken to as if it could answer back. A body learning new limits. A poet hiding behind a fan of carnations, then dissolving behind a curtain. Neat lines of script drifting over rumpled sheets: "*It's all gone now / you can turn around / whatever is left is the truth upside down.*" Each page: another way of seeing. *My Dead Flowers* feels like a shipping forecast—intangible and mysterious, familiar yet obscure, meant for those of us lost at sea, except the sea is in our heads. Pain, boredom, love, sudden hilarity trade places all day. The stakes stay close to the ground—getting out of bed; answering a phone call; crossing a street; washing one's hair; keeping a plant alive through the winter. *My Dead Flowers* never raises its voice. It sits beside you, quiet and insistent, like a bowl of dead flowers left on the table longer than decorum allows. Slowly, you realize you have begun to look at your own days a little differently.'

AKSHAY MAHAJAN

'*My Dead Flowers* feels like someone opening a window in a small room and letting air in. The photographs and text move with the softness of things noticed without hurry—a face, a corner of a house, a memory that still breathes. Nothing here is performed. Nothing is loud. There is a fragile honesty in these pages, the kind that comes only when a person is looking at the world and at themselves with equal tenderness. The images carry silence with them, and the words walk beside that silence without trying to explain it. Reading and looking through this book, I felt as if I was being trusted with something private and unpolished, something held carefully but never hidden. It is a rare experience, and a deeply human one.'

CHANDAN SAVIO GOMES

MY DEAD FLOWERS

BUKU SARKAR

FOURTH ESTATE · *New Delhi*

First published in India by Fourth Estate 2026
An imprint of HarperCollins *Publishers*
By arrangement with Thayil Ink
HarperCollins *Publishers* India, Cyber City, Building 10-A, Gurugram,
Haryana – 122002, India
www.harpercollins.co.in

2 4 6 8 10 9 7 5 3 1

P-ISBN: 978-93-6569-967-8
E-ISBN: 978-93-6569-096-5

Typeset in 11/15.5 Aldine401 BT at
HarperCollins *Publishers* India

Printed and bound at
Replika Press Pvt. Ltd.

MIX
Paper | Supporting responsible forestry
FSC™ C016779

This book is produced from independently certified FSC® paper to ensure responsible forest management.

HarperCollins *Publishers*, Macken House, 39/40 Mayor Street Upper,
Dublin 1, D01 C9W8, Ireland

For M.

Contents

An Opening Prayer	3
Coming Home	4
Wasted Years	6
For M.	7
Again for M.	8
Turn the Turn	9
False Dawn	11
You Make a Wish	13
I Woke Up Today	14
In the City of Tall Buildings	17
On Death	19
French Whispers	20
In Dreams the World Waits Its Turn	23
Nothing/Everything	25
A Tale of Tail Ends	26

I	28
Storm Song	29
True Story	30
Shop World	31
One Bourbon, One Scotch, One Beer	32
You	33
You/I	35
I Do Not Ache	37
Time Corridor	38
On Silence	39
Again, Absence	41
My Dead Flowers	43
Se Souvenir	45
A List Of	47
As Is	49
A Brief History of Pain	51
Love?	53
Love (Again)?	56
A Spurt of Magic	57

Rue St. Maur, Rue du Buisson 58
Your Porcelain Idea 59
Night for Day 62
On Serendipity 63
On Beauty 65
Day/break 66
No Good Morning 68
Lady at the Window 71
The Patient 72
Se Souvenir: Chasing Identity 77
Or Should I Go? 82
For S. 84
Winter Contract 85
Grief Is a Mother 87
Inside Out 91
Wind, Waves 93
The Nothing Variations 94
Chasing Freedom 95
Life Letter 96
Like Sunday Morning 98

The Lady in the Wheelchair	99
Magic Mirror	103
What Remains	104
To Sleep, to Dream	105
Travel and Tours	106
The Streets of Roam	107
Relationship Dilemma	111
How to See Me	112
Lone Song	114
Mon Amour with Parsley	115
Almost Prufrock	116
The Impeccable Ruins	117
All the Women Inside	118
Glass, Darkly	119
Year End	120
A Prayer to End	121
Acknowledgements	123

An Opening Prayer

What can you make of promises
That become prayers
And break?
Whatever is here, is here and nowhere else,
And so you concede.

Coming Home

It doesn't begin at the doorstep.
It begins much before,
At the familiar turn of the street,
The turn you've made every day,
At the tree,
The house at the curb,
The shops,
The windows,
The corner lights.

Home is nowhere
And nowhere is all around.

Wasted Years

I've wasted enough of my life—
Collecting clothes, books,
Specks of dust across the floor.
The things that kept vigil
Over my days,
My years.

But now it's night,
And I don't see these things anymore—
The clothes,
The books,
The dust on the floor.

I stand vigil alone,
Night-long—
So as to collect
Other things that might creep out at dark.

For M.

I love that souvenir in French
Means 'to remember'.
Like the lace handkerchief we bought together
From that shop
Next to the pet store
And that green postcard booth,
A few minutes away from Rapallo train station.

Again for M.

Yesterday is over.
But you are still here.
What will you do in its ruins?

Will you cover your face and go out again?
Will you cover every bone beneath a white sheet?
Yesterday was a disaster
So how do you live in its aftermath?
If you were a river
You could run away;
A snowflake—
You could melt;

But if you come to me,
I will colour your hair
With my warm fingers
And tell you,
I am
What you see
And all of it is yours to keep.

Turn the Turn

We start the morning paralysed,
Like stone.

Then something turns—

Reminds us of all the practical things,
And that becomes our day.
And the day after,
And the day after that.

Until you wake up years later

To realize you've taken a wrong turn somewhere—
Lost your way,
So you try and start again,
Or so you say.

False Dawn

Six in the morning,
A bus to downtown;
Walk straight up 4th Street
To the corner of Second Avenue.

The sky deep blue,
The streets, pink.
Empty sidewalks, strewn cigarette ends,
And the bar lights off.

But I know,
As I knew twenty years ago,
That behind the drawn curtains
The ashtrays are out,
The lines cut neatly on the table,
And old friends

Laugh together
Until sleep turns
To something between dawn and dusk.

They will stay there until eight, I know,
Because where else will they go?

Never home,
Never to real nightfall,
Which only draws out all the things that remain
Hidden during the day.

You Make a Wish

Like snowflakes in July,
                    softly,
In case someone hears.
(It won't come true.)

You can't wish for everything,
Because there's too much to ask for.

So you ask for one small thing and wait.

But after the wish is made,
You speak only to the gardenias
At the window.

I Woke Up Today

And you weren't there.
I woke up yesterday, and then too.
Last month,
Last year,
The year before.

It's confusing because you're here—
Your hand poised under your chin,
In thought
Or pretence thought.
And we are bitching about Emily and Wallace,
But also the aunt next door.

I don't think of you always, but you're there,
Present, yet absently,
Like the sofa or the cat.

Like that tree in your courtyard with serpentine roots,
Which has witnessed many afternoons
Through the gap in your curtain,
When we sat on the bed you were born on
And bitched not just about Emily and Wallace
But also K and C and A.

I will not call you the next time I'm in town,
Or on my next return, or the visit after.
Some other time perhaps.
Because you'll be there.
Just like you always are.
And we have always spent our time together leisurely,
Without urgency and obligation.
Only when we wanted.
And you said,
B, I wish I had your courage to say no to others
And hide in my own world like you do.
You said that before you went to the hospital.
You said that years ago.
So see, you're still here. Only in hiding.

In the City of Tall Buildings

Everything changes.
Everything remains.

One's only hope was to remain a spectator.

Mistakes had been made.
Prayers spit back.
He said these words—words that he had always believed
    like a prayer—
Even as they collapsed, syllable by syllable, all over his
    pillowcase each night.
His life was nothing but a progression of denials.
He'd wasted it here, in this small corner of the city,
And in doing so, he'd ruined it everywhere else.
Behind the Ramble,
Lost in the woods,
Walking on wooden bridges over little streams.

But if he strained his eyes to the west,
He could see high-rises.
They hovered over the horizon—life's guarantee.

On Death

Death never really went away.
It was not an ending.
Memory itself was a constant reminder
Of something no longer present.

French Whispers

What would we be, each to each,
If there was no 'we'
Between you and I?

Then there'd be
No agneau au cumin
We ate yesterday,
Or the shrimp soup
You cooked the night before
Because I wasn't well.

There'd be no whispers in French
Asking me to move over
Because you're almost out of the bed,
And that je tombe du lit
Has a different euphemistic meaning
Than what AI has been telling me.

I ask AI: *What would life be without M. in it?*
It answers:
That depends—who is M. to you?
A friend, a partner, a pet, a mentor?
Sounds like they're important to you,
So I imagine life would feel different—
Maybe emptier, maybe freer,
Maybe just … different.

What makes you wonder about this?

So, I changed the M. to Mon amour, and now it tells me:
If 'Mon amour' is someone you deeply love,
Then life without them would likely feel like a huge shift—
Maybe quieter, maybe lonelier,
Maybe just missing a certain warmth and familiarity.
Love has a way of shaping our world,
Filling spaces we don't even realize until they're empty.

Are you asking this out of curiosity,
Or is something on your mind?

If there was no 'we' between you and I,
Who would I tell this to
Tomorrow?

A friend?
Who wouldn't just say,
Hmm,
Not in your Arab accent, but French—perhaps a little Arab mixed—
Maybe half-and-half, forty-five–fifty-five

Mon amour,
There can never be no 'we' between us.
That was the answer I wanted—from you,
From the computer.

In Dreams the World Waits Its Turn

Under three blankets
The dogs breathe.
I will have to wait till sunrise
To run to your apartment,
A few doors down,
And while I wait,
I dream,
        And in my dream
        We are a we.

Not the kind of we I hate. But *we.*
You and me.
We only to you and to me
In privacy.

To the rest of the world—
let them be.

In my dream,
Somewhere out there,
Is a we
Who are still each for each.

And when a dream is so real,
How can it be anything else?

Nothing/Everything

Bright sun,
White snow,
Crystal snow.

Nothing's wrong.

Then maybe the departure—
A blue sky,
White clouds,
Cotton clouds,
Clouds with silver.

Still nothing wrong—
Then what's all this about?

A Tale of Tail Ends

I

Write to you
When
I
Write.

Not
Of you,
But to you;

So you
May
Remember
Everything I
Never said.

Storm Song

The storm winds
Bring with them
Memories
From another land;

Then which song is mine—
The one that comes in or the one that recedes?

True Story

The stories that have been written down
Are not the real stories.

The real stories
Are the softest
And faintest sound
In your mind.

Always unsaid.

Shop World

Trudging on.
The cracked sidewalks that led to the shops.
The shops that led to the avenue.
The shops that led to home.
The shops that were his world.

One Bourbon, One Scotch, One Beer

Penny for your thoughts, you say.
A bottle of whiskey for yours.
After all, after the holiday pictures have been uploaded,
what else is there to say?
Let's sit across a small wooden table, with uncomfortable
chairs;
Maybe one of those rare finds where they still let you
smoke inside and drink a toast to never.

You

You,

Quiet.

Stay home. Swipe the screen.

Order groceries online for 5 p.m.

Go to a café with your laptop

As you wait.

The snow comes down in crystals.

You

Swipe and scroll

And sift.

The road will be clear in fifteen minutes,

Says the app.

The little things in life.

On your way out,

Read something on your phone.

You

Don't look ahead because the snow has wiped out the streets.

You

Come home.
Pour a glass of wine,
Or whisky,
Depending on which country you live in.
Turn on the news on the television;
The phone makes a sound.
Mute the television.
Soon the alarm will go off
Reminding you it's an hour until bedtime.

You

Want peace
And quiet,
Away from all this noise.

You

You.
Yes, you.

You/I

You know what I hate about you?
That you can tell when I'm pretending.
But I've gone through half of my life this way,
Now what am I supposed to do?

I Do Not Ache

I would not trade this life
For any other.
I thought happiness was only a myth,
So I never expected.
And
So
I
Am.

And did I get what I wanted,
The keeper of life's secrets,
The keeper of its ruins?

They tell you to love yourself.
I tell them I already do.

Time Corridor

Time passes by us,
Or do we pass by time
As people who forget?

Was it
In yesterday's present
And the one not yet arrived?

In that corridor
Walk our myths.

On Silence

Listen to it
Coming in through
The window.
The single tree cries to keep living;
The wind howls to say your name.

These things must happen,
When everything else purports to sleep, for only when
it's quiet
Do I speak,
So you can listen, completely.
It's the way I've arranged the world for you.

The wind will whisper little secrets,
And we, who listen to the wind,

Shall see this year and
The one that passed last week.

We shall sit on this earth,
And the rain
Will wash our tears.
The world's soft tears will speak.

Again, Absence

I love:
The smell of oranges from the cake in the oven,
The white noise of your radio,
Fresh laundry in the small closet next to the bathroom.

Vegetables stewing
While you pick at the parsley.

Your black shirt, not laundered.
Your hair, unwashed.
The moods of seven days
Drizzled in it, like oil.

And because these thoughts
Constantly follow me,

I follow them back,
And wait for portents.

And because none of these things exist,
I love them even more.

And because there is no you,
I stay with your absence.

My Dead Flowers

You see the hardy jasmine by the wall?
We had to replace the climbing roses last winter.
And the gardenias all died,
So we planted camellias instead.
The annuals are long gone.
And I never understood the point
Of planting something that
Doesn't live year-round.
I mean, all that hard work,
When you know it will perish anyway—

What sense does that make?

I'm not lazy, I'm not lazy at all,
I give everything, I do my all;

But just so they can survive,
To remind me that despite everything
Some things do stay,
Year to year,
Like the hardy jasmine
Next to the camellias.
One flowers in the summer,
The other in the winter;
Each complementing the other.

Se Souvenir

Things that are meant to be lost:
        Lighters,
              Hair clasps,
                    Socks,
                          Scissors,
                                        Passports—only when you need it,
                                                Lists,
                         Your favourite dress,
                  Time,
        Names,
The feel of your skin.
        Keys,

Streets,
Directions,
Wooden spoons—the kind you greased over years,
Words,
Faces,
Husbands,
Countries,
Apartments,
Photo frames,
My favourite tart pan

Which somehow got mixed with your things.

A List Of

Ideas
Dreams
Goals
Tasks
Groceries
Appointments
Holidays
Plans
Music
Recipes
Birthdays
Film screenings
Theatre listings
Dinners
Resolutions
The droplets of water leaking from the ceiling
Friends

People who aren't friends anymore
Acquaintances
Semi-acquaintances
Phone calls you muted
Bus timings
Train schedules
Doorbells you didn't answer
Luggage
Quaint hotels in Italy
Restaurants
Books to read
Books never to read
The number of light bulbs you need
Stationery, so you can start writing by hand again
(Like one ought to)
Days before you have to wash your hair again
Days till you must bathe again
Lovers
Departures

And a list of the ones who slipped away.

As Is

Why do you cry
When you have no leaves?
    Do you not see your body,
    Bare to the bruised bones
    Yet so pristine?
    Do you not celebrate
    Your hard scars?

Your many tentacles hanging low
Or standing straight;
Your spine serpentine,
Your perfect shape
In all its shapes.

So simple.

A brocade with no beginning

And no end.

You wear nothing
As you stand,
Dance,
Whisper,
Lightly graze yourself.

Be naked,
Beautiful.
Be maskless.
Be that you are
As yourself,
By yourself.

A Brief History of Pain

I live with the freedom of solitude,
Bound only by the ways of the wind.
Singing the song of the season—
And when things quiet down,
I, too, settle.

Love?

I love you, I say.
Je t'aime aussi, you say.

Pour quoi? I ask.
(I can't even walk.)

Because of the thing up there—
You point at the ceiling,
Even though you don't believe in god.

Our wine was almost done,
But I could not finish the tortilla.
I was hoping I wouldn't fall while walking back home,
Or worse, get another comment from a passerby—ça va?

The pharmacy light at the corner of Rue St. Maur
And Rue du Buisson St. Louis was still lit—
The corner of your street and mine.

What is love? I shout,
When you are across the street
On the small square with empty benches,
Where they sell cheap bread for the homeless—
Still a few feet away from the Tunisian coiffeur.

It's everything you've ever believed,
But it's nothing you can ever say.

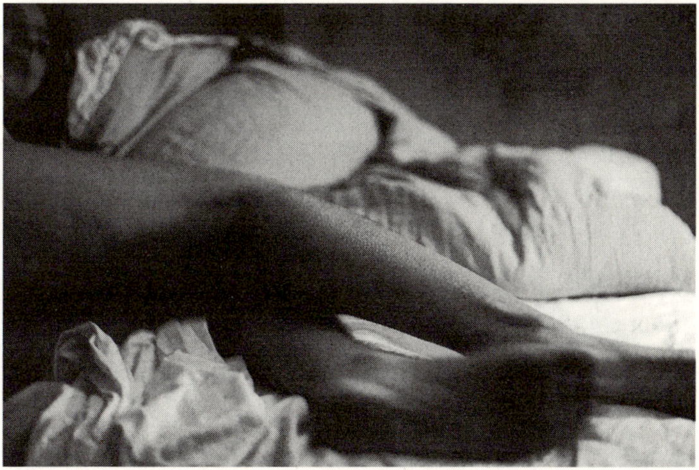

Love (Again)?

I'm looking at a photo
That is supposed to change my morning.

The crow flies across the screen.

It is July on the clock,
The beginning of the end—

Isn't it always?

I love you more than the word.

A Spurt of Magic

Not so fast, my love,
Let time be.
Don't you know we caught it:
Between you and I,
We live between now and eternity.

Magic happens in spurts,
Not like the flowing river,
But slowly,
            like afternoon rain.

Nothing lasts forever, remember.
Let's save this until it happens again.

Rue St. Maur, Rue du Buisson

The corner of Rue St. Maur and Rue du Buisson always
        felt like the edge of an abyss,
Because you lived there, so it had to be where all
        wonderful things began and ended.
But the view from its periphery is
No less obscure.
There is no secret after the big plunge.
The corner of our two streets, the old man at the green
        café who doesn't like me,
All remind me of something bigger,
Remind me that I once was alive, because of you,

Your Porcelain Idea

Sometimes, I think
I'm just an idea that people like.

For example:
My childhood best friend likes the idea of me so much
That when I visit London,
Every other year or so,
He never makes an attempt to meet me for dinner.
Instead, he makes me come to his house in the west of
the city,
Where one can reach without saying one lives in the
suburbs,
And makes me watch Indian news with him.

I'm like the sofa or the cat. You only notice me when I'm
gone.
But you don't mourn for too long.

For example:
My father loves me dearly, but always cuts our phone
conversations short.
And my twin only asks if it is an emergency, else she is
busy.

It's not that they don't love me.
But perhaps I'm that fine thing that ages well with
storage.
And when I'm back in New York or Paris, wherever
home happens to be,
Not in the same city as them,
I'm ageing gracefully until our next meeting.

Which is not a terrible idea of its own,
An idea that is ageing.

Then I don't grieve so much about just being an idea to
my loved ones.
Because I know that they know that I know—
And that's enough.

My only regret is that I'm not made of porcelain.
That would've been a precious idea.

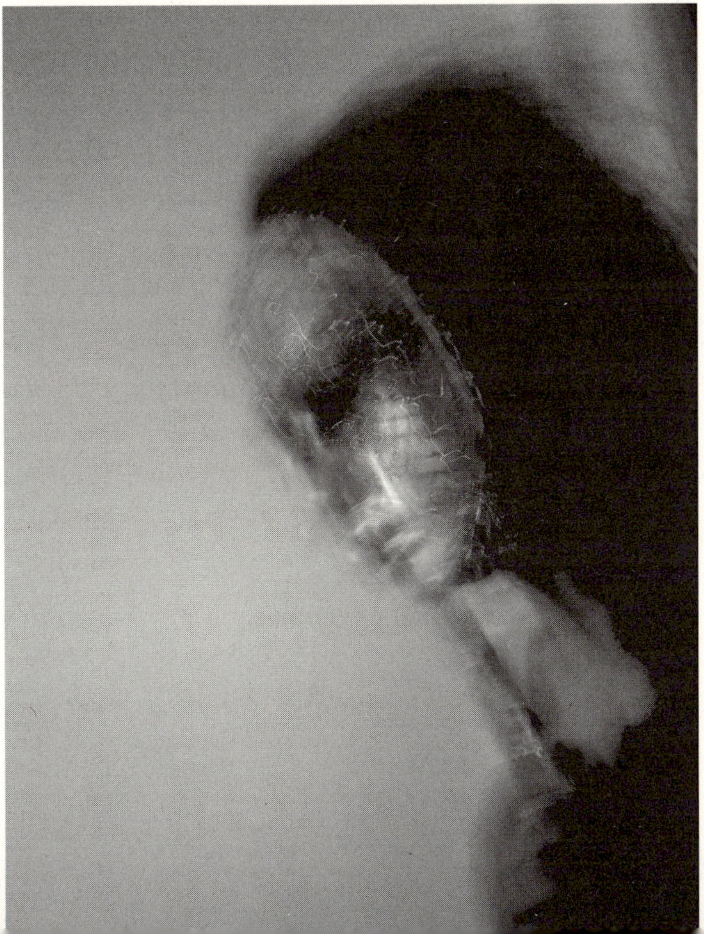

Night for Day

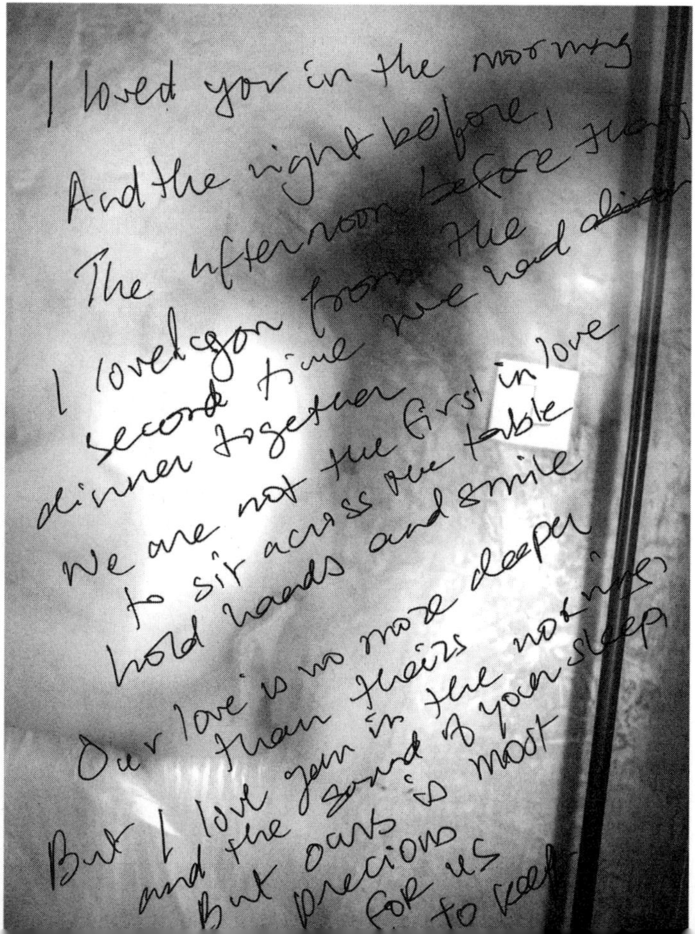

On Serendipity

'I'm moving in with someone I met.'
It was so simple.
I should have said it yesterday. But I couldn't.
Instead I went on about serendipity,
Gave the man hope,
Long after I'd left his city, his country.
I didn't mean to be cruel.

It felt better than the physical pleasure I hadn't felt
—two drinks after we met at the café—
When I let him into my hotel room—my suitcase still on
the bed
For extra neck brace.

Later, I thought, what a waste of time.

But his cry of ecstasy;
The tears on his face—

I gave him something that night.

I hope, even now, if not me,
Someone else is watching him from the street,
As he cups his chin by a half-drawn curtain,
Waiting for another drink
At another café.

On Beauty

The morning was devastating,
So beautiful, it was almost sad.

Because you knew there could never be anything
More perfect than this.

That this was where it all began,
And ended.
On that bench,
With a single ray of light
Weaving its way through the cracks of leaves
And dispersing all over the green wood;

A sadness more uplifting than joy
Because sadness pierces,
And with that piercing comes a change that is new.

Day/break

Nobody told me I was beautiful today—
What life am I waking up to?
Do I have to wake up at all?
On whose orders can I not stay hidden in these grey folds
That look so pretty in a picture,
If taken from an angle
Without the coffee stain
From last year?

No.
Yes—

Last year.

Just after the accident
When I'd drink coffee in bed.

In the afternoons, the bed turned into a sofa, and at
night,
A place my eyes saw as darkness,
Only to realize it's daybreak again.

Why do they say that—daybreak?
Who is it that already knows
What I must find out?

For the moment, I am part of these linen folds
Where, when I close my eyes,
Anything is possible.

Until I remember—

Day
break

It broke something that was perfectly fine.

No Good Morning

Why must we say *good morning*?
What if it's a bad morning?
A terrible morning?

What if I haven't slept at all?
Has the night passed?

How different the morning looks
To one who has risen

Than to one who has just staggered home.

Time is the same whether you stay awake
Or drink—
It stops or slips away.

I can't say *good morning*,
Not if I'm pure and good and honest—

And isn't that the point?

Instead, we start our days with lies
And build this tangled web,
And count the remaining time
Against the beat of a ghostly drum.

Lady at the Window

Who are you,
Lady at the window?

Are you dancing your dreams
Or do you carry the world on your shoulders?

The Patient

Sunday:
Kadhi chawal

Kadhi chawal recipe in Bengali—Google search

Note: minimize oil and no chilli

Apple purée with chena and raisin and cinnamon
Doodh jhinge

She has passed stool, which is a good sign
Parameters have not deteriorated
No fluid in lungs

Monday:
Soup with chicken kofta and spinach and rice
Momo plus steamed lauki/carrot
Custard apple purée

Talking, which is good, but not bossing, which I'm not sure is good or bad

Evening, breaking news: Dr G.D. said he is cautiously optimistic

She sat on a chair to have her meal and complained bitterly how the hospital food has deteriorated

Is there a difference between a present and a gift?

When his eldest daughter was getting married, Brunello Cucinelli knew exactly what to get her: not just one gift, but a thousand-book library filled with texts that had inspired him. 'With this, I believe I have made both a present, which is largely a physical thing, and a gift, which is a more spiritual gesture.'

Tuesday:
Congee made with chicken stock and chicken pieces

How to make congee video in Hindi—Google search

Dalia khichdi plus steamed sheem

Dalia khichdi Bengali—Google search

The nurse said she sat on a chair and had coconut water
which is high in potassium
In the afternoon she walked around her bed a little
She said quality of sponging a patient—a hallmark of
excellence with old Anglo-Indian or Malayali
nurses—is sadly missing
Abdominal pain has vastly reduced but infection persists

X owner Elon Musk appears to be spooked by the
number of users leaving the social media
platform in favour of alternatives like Bluesky.
Source: Futurism

Wednesday:
Light machher jhol with fish fillet rice

They wheeled her downstairs for a CT scan

In the afternoon, she saw me and said: 'I look like Yoda'
(Ha. Ha. Part of my job is to be Yoda.)

Have you opened a bank account at BNP yet?

Dandadan on Netflix—try

Thursday:
Phena bhaat with shreds of chicken, whites of egg and
vegetables, carrots and zucchini

She's looking more and more like her mother

Beauty is mysterious as well as terrible. God and the devil are fighting there, and the battlefield is the heart of man.
DOSTOEVSKY

Friday:
No meal planned as she says she can't tolerate the bedpan
any more
What a catastrophe
Whom do I cook for now?

But she saw me and took a poop

Lungs a little stressed but stable otherwise
Still on oxygen

Yes, she must stay in the ICU
The round-the-clock medical care and attention one gets
there is more important than having visitors

Re: your question:
Real happiness can never be remembered

Se Souvenir: Chasing Identity

When Instagram banned my account, I stayed in bed for
seven days.
Someone from the World Wide Web,
Whose face I had never seen,
Told me they knew a person who could retrieve it.
This person's number was in Indonesia, said Google.

This person tells me I have to pay him first.
How? I ask.
He sends me a link to a website that sells game cards
In denominations of $50. 'Three,' he says.
It takes me a while because the website
Sends me a verification email. Then another.
Confirming identity is never-ending.

‘But your Instagram account is in the highest security,’
He tells me later.
He needs more advanced software to bypass the security,
Which means more payments.

This time the website doesn’t allow me access.
So he sends me to another, which rejects my payment.

The Indonesian says he will take bitcoins too.
Does one draw them from an ATM like cash?

While I don’t know this world anymore,
I do know there is a game shop half a mile away,
where they sell those cards.

But I’m disabled, I whine,
When he asks me to hurry there.
I cringe that I use that word ‘but’ in moments of calamity.
It works.

People shut up.
Normally, I'd have said:
I'm doing much better. I see the silver lining.

But not to the Indonesian.
Time is of utmost urgency.

So I go …
I don't know how.
When you're determined, you can do anything, I suppose.
A. taught me that.

In the end, of course, it doesn't work.
I lose three hundred dollars,
I lose my Instagram account, which took years to build.

I call him a liar.
He calls me a witch.

I just laugh and save the conversation to write a short
story about later on—a notebook full of ideas—
which I never look at again

First, I know I'd have to ward off the faint for days.

Then, I might have to call the acupuncturist;
Because the doctors have done nothing.
Then, I'll have to figure out how to get
To the kitchen to heat soup.
And finally, when courage runs out, I just have to take
the plunge—
Figure out how to be
In this
Real world.

Or Should I Go?

Silk roses
And a leopard-skin rug.

A pleather sofa in burgundy.

You told me to come
And I did,
Though it took a year.

I sit here with a drink in my hand,
Poured from a gallon container,
And don't know what to say.

We are from the same country,
But we speak different languages.
We always have.
That's how our country raised us.

You on this side,
I on the other.

I am the first to arrive,
Which is a relief.
But once the others appear,
I lose the few words I remember.

I am that awkward lady in the corner
Standing by herself,
Although I know you're looking from the edge of your
eye.

But the saddest truth is:
You see me with a smile and a glass of wine,
Leaning into all edges of my pure cashmere pants,
And you, in your simplicity and unawareness,
Are so relieved by the fact that I came,
You don't realize
I've been checking the time
Every other minute.

For S.

You caught me by the hand and pulled me away
To the verandah,
Away from the cutting cake, the claps. You said:
Will you watch the day go by with me?

Your smile was a blanket between monsoon and
The winter yet to come.

You were five then.

The tree in your name is now eight.

Time has stopped,
Wisdom will die,
But I'll always have a song for you.

Winter Contract

Spring is an anticipation
Of all the new things
To come.
                    Summer—a celebration,
                    Like moist skin after sex.

But winter is remembrance
And loss.

Carcasses of trees,
Baring
Their real figures,
Their real curves.

Like a naked woman
Who has lost everything.

And is no longer afraid.

Once you've stood in a park
With no clothes,
You can do anything.

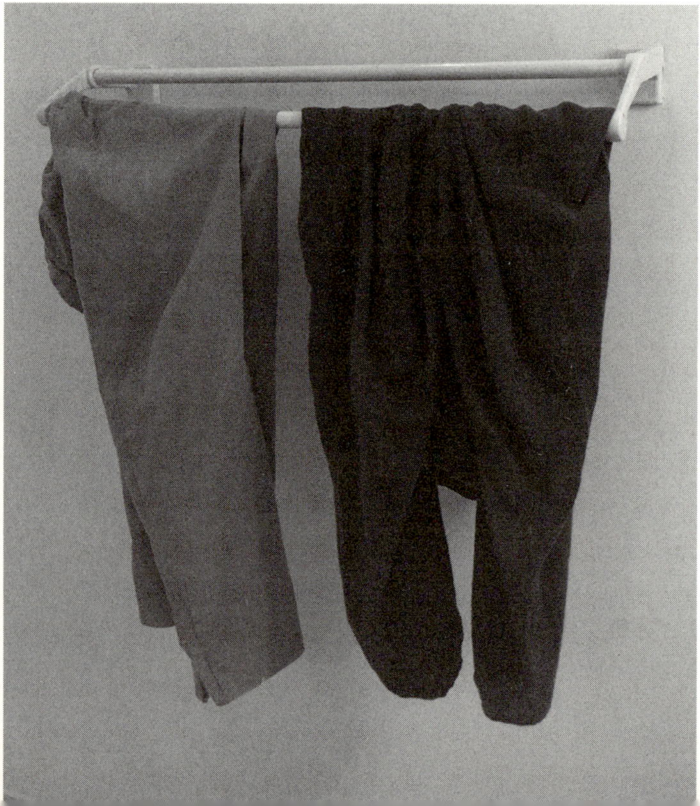

Grief Is a Mother

If you're so full of grief
That it swells over your face,
Fills every corner of your neck and chest and abdomen;

If you're so full of grief
That you're bloated,
You can't even drown;

(And dust from ten thousand dreams
Keeps you afloat);

So full of grief are you
That you're a vessel of misery,
A walking-talking sculpture of ruins;

(You could collapse any moment
And yet you've become so hard
It's impossible
            to collapse anymore.)

You are grief.
That's all you are.

And the funny thing is,
No one even notices.

So, outside, you are a thing,
And inside, you're a wretch.

How does one live in such a state?

Because it's too late—
You are stone,
A grotesquely shaped rock.

Waves crash in and out every evening,
Chipping at it
Pinch by pinch,

And in a thousand years,
Its stain will still remain.

So invisible is your grief,
And so enduring.

And no one notices
On the streets;
And no one notices
Over the phone,
Or at the pharmacy,
Or the Chinese takeaway.

Except me.

You can't fool me.
You could never fool me.
That's how I knew that I was for you—

So I could take the grief from your face
And warm it in my two hands.

Nothing will be okay,
But I can carry some of your grief

And perhaps slowly,
I can take on more,
And you can take on less,
And your grief will melt in my palm
And on my skin.

Is it too late?
Is it?
No one knows.

But I can wipe away the tears
Trickling down;

I can come in the evening
And pour grief out of you
Like wastewater from a large vessel;

Wipe it gently from the corners of your lips
Like vomit.

I love you so well.

Inside Out

The great tree
Stands outside my bedroom.
Its green and brown
Turned inside out,
Making holes in
The cement of the wall
Like a great ache
In the heart.

It sees me climb the gate
Quietly,
Past sleeping guards,
When the lights outside houses
Light up the night.

My heels trying to find
The same fastenings
Its roots once did.

The great tree
Has stood vigil,
But unlike our guards,
Those twenty-some years ago,
Does not climb over my open balcony
Into my bed.

It sees me lock my door,
And hears the timid
Piano notes of my trembling fingers,
When what I feel has no name.

And it shakes silver when caught in the rain.

If it spoke,
It would say:

Won't you come out
Ever again?

Wind, Waves

Just as the wind leaves no scar
On the river,
So too do you stir me
With your touch.

Just like the wind and the waves do
All night,
We turn and touch,
And rise and touch.

And in the morning,
We meet again.

The Nothing Variations

Days slipped away,
Nothing
But variations of sunlight
Hitting brick walls.

Cries outside the window
Like an interruption in time,

And the wind
And the rain
Shattering down.

Nothing's worse than morning.

Chasing Freedom

We stop through little towns
On our way to Jerez.
You get out of the car for beer,
I, for a cigarette.
You turn to me,
You say, 'Ça va?'
And all I can do is smile my answer.
As simple as that.

Life Letter

Sometimes, every day feels like a rehearsal for the next.

Just because you know the life
You are meant to live is not this one,
But one yet to come.

So let's just bugger this day.

Because this is not a life
Just as this is not a prayer;
And I'm not writing this.

Then, beautiful world, where are you?
I've been waiting so long
For you to arrive,

Like the weather;
Like truth.

What would you say if you saw us?
What would you say if you had your left fist raised?

Dear Life,
We were waiting,
We were waiting,
But you were always there, just as lost as us.

Like Sunday Morning

The grey from the walls merges with
The grey from the skies,
Which is part of a grey much larger.
How much of the world
Is in a man?

The Lady in the Wheelchair

It's midday.
The flight was supposed to be at ten.
I've already read two poems on vanilla ice cream.

When? I asked myself.
Any time now.

I want to go home.

But then what?
What happens once you arrive at your destination?

What waits on the other side?

Answer.

When?
Shh.

What happens is everything,
And that is nothing.
Every
Nothing.

I turned to the old woman
On my left
Whose grey braided hair
Was lost behind her back
As she sat in her wheelchair.

I smiled.

The lady had been sitting quietly,
But she seemed to like this interference.

No one wants to sit inside
Their thoughts all day.

She smiled back,
And in that smile
I understood
Everything that once was,
Still is,
And will be.

Magic Mirror

I raise the mirror of my life
To my face,
And throw at the reflection
The crystal ashtray
I never had any use for.

There, all is in place now.

What Remains

Every rooftop the sun touches,
Every tree,
Side lane,
Corner shop;

Every pot it captures for a few moments,
Every tea cup
And bowl,

Is a reminder
There's nothing left.

To Sleep, to Dream

We dream to sleep and sleep to dream.
It is time to know
Nothing again,
All over again.

These dreams are old,
I need new ones—

 If I can't erase my memories,
 Who will I be tomorrow?

We think in yesterday,
And live in tomorrow,
And the rest of the time
We dream.

 So, give me a new dream.
 Isn't that what living is all about?

Travel and Tours

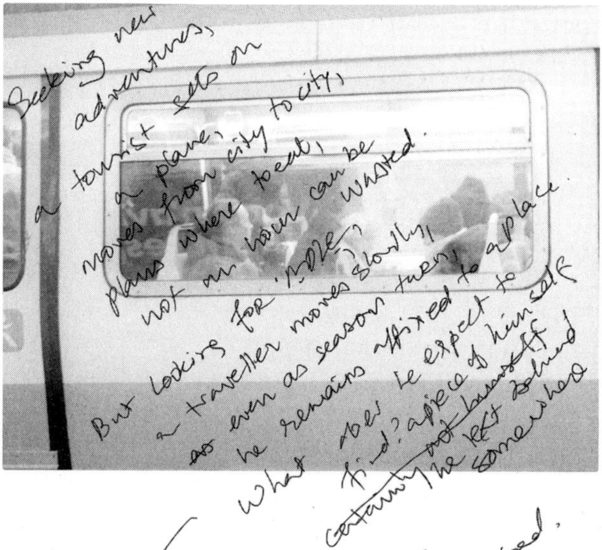

Seeking new
adventures,
a tourist ~~sets~~ on
a plane,
moves from city to city,
plans where to eat,
not an hour can be
wasted.

But looking for 'more',
a traveller moves slowly,
~~as~~ even as season turns,
he remains affixed to a place.
What does he expect to
find? a piece of himself
~~certainty~~ he left behind
somewhere

he eats at the
same places,
sleeps on the same bed,
but he is never home.
He is always
looking

The Streets of Roam

The streets I roam
Open out the moment I say
Good Morning to the doorman and make a turn.

The streets I roam can go either way—
Left to the fancy bakery or right
To the 84th Street entrance of the park.

If I turn left to go to the bakery,
I make it a point to stop by Mrs Kim's,
Where the croissant is too dry, and the pastries a few days old.
I hug her and ask about her daughters.
Sometimes, the man behind the counter sings a song for me.
He has the voice of a classically trained singer.

If I turn right on the streets where I roamed—
It was when S. was still alive.
We would walk three avenue blocks,
Right in front of the Metropolitan Museum
And a small entrance to the park.

Dodging the other dogs whom we both found a menace,
We would head straight to the Rambles.

At six there was no one anywhere,
And S. chased squirrels freely
While I pondered the ending to my next story.

Once, a squirrel took her to the edge of the pond
And unable to slow down, she fell in.
I should have tried to save her, but I laughed instead—
Looking at the expression on her face.

(I am very calm during a crisis.)

If you don't look up at the horizon, you're no longer in the city.
Then it's all mine—
The sidewalks, the turtle pond,
The mini wooden bridges over the whispering water.

I know which tree comes next, which bench,
Which garbage can is by the entrance.

But, I have long forgotten the dry cleaning lady's name;
Or, at least, I cannot recall it today—
The woman who would give S. a treat
Every morning at six before we went out,
For eight years.

Then I feel I have lost everything.

The condition with which I left the city
Was that everything would still be waiting for me
When I decided to return.

I know,
When the plane touches the tarmac
It will all come back.

I'm more at ease now. With myself.

Jessie! That's her name.

All I have to do is think of a plane

And my entirety is already in the streets I roamed.
No one knows me anymore—
Jessie closed her shop;
The man with the eyepatch and blind dog has moved;
So have all the renters in my old building.
But the streets where I used to roam look the same—

Despite the French patisserie,
The German patisserie,
The new Italian restaurant.

I still roam them every night
When the rest of the house is asleep.
And I sometimes think—
What have I done?

Sappho once wrote:
'What cannot be said will be wept.'

Relationship Dilemma

Girls, I have a problem that you might help me with.

I met a man recently—
He's smart, he knows how to make me feel special—
The only problem is, he is three inches shorter than me.

Have you ever been with a man who is shorter than you?
What are the downsides?

Thanks for all your help.

How to See Me

View me as large,
View me small,
In megapixels,
In high definition,
In AI,
Algorithms,
In Photoshop,
And in a programme that makes all my nightmares go away,
So I can be happy and smiling for you.

View me as an attachment,
View me as a post,
View me as a video,
And then you can dream of me at night—
Not the way you imagined,
Nor I,

But with crystal clarity, so pure,
We are no longer you and me
But a pristine promise.

Lone Song

A penny for your thoughts, my sweet?
Let's walk to the water—
For a little dance, a sad song;

We will talk till every crumb of yesterday
Is over.

We say goodbye
The way people do
When they've not known each other
For too long.

Mon Amour with Parsley

We may have a lifetime before us,
But that is still not enough time.

So please take longer in picking the parsley,
And looking for your glasses,
And let a few plates fall
From last night's dinner,
So we can kneel down together,
With yesterday's headache,
And say: what a laugh!

Almost Prufrock

Let us meet,
You and I,
In our dreams—
Halfway from mine,
Halfway to yours,

And you can tell me all about today
While I learn your English;

So that, by the end of the night,
I can give you something to hold and wake up to.

The Impeccable Ruins

So how does it feel
To stand in its ruins now?
When we had so impeccably planned
Every plane ticket, hotel room, holiday, dog sitter?

The broken bits hurt my feet, you say.

You see?

That was always the problem.

All the Women Inside

Glass, Darkly

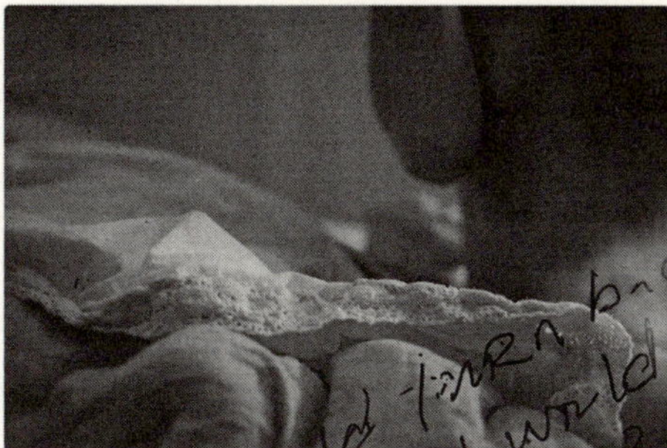

If I could turn back,
What ~~should~~ would I want
behind me?
A mirror, so I can
easily see?
Or darkness, through
which I must walk
closed eyes?

Year End

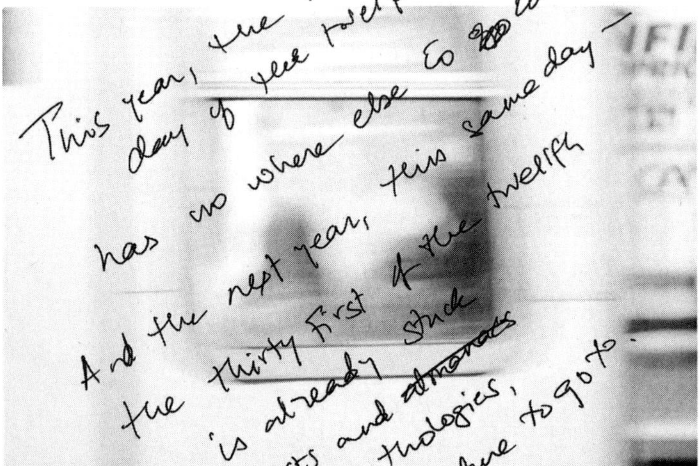

This year, the thirty-first
day of the twelfth month,
has no where else to come to,
And the next year, this same day —
the thirty first of the twelfth
is already stuck
in lists and
and anthologies,
it has no future to go to.

A Prayer to End

Because there are always two endings
To a story,
I felt I learned to lose you
Long before I learned to love you.

ACKNOWLEDGEMENTS

Once one starts 'acknowledgements', they never end, so I'll keep this short and simple: I wanted to say thank you to Jeet for trusting me and making me trust myself.

ABOUT THE AUTHOR

Buku Sarkar is a photographer and writer who works between Calcutta, New York, and Paris. Her writing has appeared in *The New York Review of Books*, *n+1*, *ZYZZYVA* and *The Threepenny Review*, while her photography has been featured in *The New York Times* and *Art Miami* and has been exhibited at the International Center of Photography.

Buku Sarkar has been a recipient of the Andrew Lytle Best Short Story Award (2021). Her debut novel, *Not Quite a Disaster After All*, was published by HarperCollins India in 2023 and is now available in the US with Flowersong Press. Her photobook, *Photowali Didi* (Fall Line Press, 2023), documenting her five-year relationship with residents of a Calcutta slum, explores themes of identity and belonging across cultures.

Buku Sarkar serves as part-time faculty at the International Center of Photography and offers writing workshops.

Her screenplay *The Shameless* was adapted into a feature film that premiered at the Cannes Film Festival's Un Certain Regard section in 2024. Her work examines the complexities of cross-cultural identity, feminine freedom, social stratification and the spaces between worlds—both literal and metaphorical. She is currently working on a novel about two generations of an Indian family in New York, a memoir about living with a neurological disorder, endless short stories, and a photographic series exploring women's relationships with their bodies—building on seven years of documenting her own illness through self-portraits in the series 'Containment Diaries'.

HarperCollins *Publishers* India

At HarperCollins India, we believe in telling the best stories and finding the widest readership for our books in every format possible. We started publishing in 1992; a great deal has changed since then, but what has remained constant is the passion with which our authors write their books, the love with which readers receive them, and the sheer joy and excitement that we as publishers feel in being a part of the publishing process.

Over the years, we've had the pleasure of publishing some of the finest writing from the subcontinent and around the world, including several award-winning titles and some of the biggest bestsellers in India's publishing history. But nothing has meant more to us than the fact that millions of people have read the books we published, and that somewhere, a book of ours might have made a difference.

As we look to the future, we go back to that one word—a word which has been a driving force for us all these years.

Read.

Harper Collins | Harper Sport | HARPER FICTION | HARPER NON-FICTION | हार्पर हिन्दी

HARPER LEARNING | HARPER VANTAGE | HCCB HARPERCOLLINS CHILDREN'S BOOKS | 4th | HARPER PERENNIAL

HARPER DESIGN | BOOKTOPUS | HARPER BUSINESS